COLLINS GEM GUIDES

THE NIGHT SKY

illustrations by
Wil Tirion

text by
Ian Ridpath

D1079632

COLLINS
London and Glasgow

Cover Photograph: the beautiful Helix Nebula, NGC 7293, in the constellation of Aquarius. *Anglo-Australian Telescope Board.*

Opposite: the Whirlpool Galaxy in the constellation of Canes Venatici.

First published 1985

© Ian Ridpath and Wil Tirion 1985

ISBN 0 00 458817 7

Colour reproduction by Anglia Reproductions, Witham, Essex

Filmset by Ace Filmsetting Ltd, Frome, Somerset

Printed and bound by Wm Collins Sons & Co Ltd, Glasgow

Reprint 10 9 8 7 6 5 4 3 2 1

Contents

How to use this Book

This book contains individual charts of the 88 constellations that fill the entire sky (in alphabetical order). All the stars marked on the charts are visible to the naked eye under clear skies, but in towns, where the skies are polluted by dirt and the glare from streetlights, binoculars may be necessary to pick out the faintest stars shown. In addition to the naked-eye stars, the maps mark the location of other important objects such as star clusters, nebulae and galaxies; most of these require some form of optical aid to be seen. Specific areas of interest in certain constellations (such as the Pleiades, page 213), are shown in greater detail on larger-scale maps which include fainter stars than on the main charts.

Each constellation chart is accompanied by descriptions of the main objects of interest to the amateur observer, with an indication of the type of instrument and the magnification needed to see them. The majority of objects described are within the range of small telescopes (i.e. telescopes whose front lens has an aperture of 50–60 mm).

The position of the constellations in relation to each other can be found from a ten-page mini-atlas of the entire sky on pages 28–37.

This book is usable anywhere in the world, although not all constellations will be visible from any given place, e.g. constellations in the south polar region of the sky will always remain below the horizon for mid-northern latitude observers, and vice versa.

Introduction

The sky is divided up into 88 areas, known as *constellations*, which serve as a convenient way of locating the position of objects in the sky. The stars of a constellation usually have no physical connection between one another: although they appear in the same direction in the sky, they are actually at vastly differing distances from us.

Constellations come in many different shapes and sizes. The largest constellation, Hydra, the water snake, is a long and rambling figure that covers an area of sky 19 times greater than that of the smallest constellation, Crux, the southern cross. Some constellations consist of easily recognizable patterns of bright stars, such as Orion, while others are faint and difficult to identify.

The tradition of dividing the sky into constellations began thousands of years ago when ancient peoples assigned certain star patterns the names of their gods, heroes and fabled animals. With few exceptions, the star patterns bear very little resemblance to the people and creatures they are supposed to represent; the connections are symbolic rather than literal.

The ancient Greeks recognized a total of 48 constellations, including the 12 constellations of the *zodiac*, through which the Sun passes on its yearly path around the sky. (The Sun's path, known as the *ecliptic*, is plotted on the maps in this book as a dashed line.) Various other constellations were added at later times.

Early celestial cartographers drew the constellation figures as they pleased, for there was no standardized shape for each one, nor was there even a generally agreed list of constellations. Each cartographer was free to introduce new constellations of his own invention, and to amend or omit the inven-

Quadrans Muralis, an old constellation that once occupied a place above the head of Boötes, as shown on the 1801 star atlas of Johann Bode. *Royal Greenwich Observatory.*

tions of others. Constellation figures frequently overlapped one another, and sometimes stars were shared between two constellations.

This state of confusion persisted until 1930 when the International Astronomical Union, astronomy's governing body, adopted the list of 88 constellations that we know today, and set down their exact boundaries. There is no particular reason why we should have 88 constellations, or why they should be the shape they are. Rather like the political map of the world, the subdivision of the sky is an accident of history. But unlike the countries of the world, the names and the borders of the constellations are not likely to change until the slow, steady movements of the stars, known as their *proper motions*, render the existing constellation shapes unrecognizable, thousands of years from now.

Star brightnesses

Star brightnesses are expressed in terms of *magnitudes* (abbreviated mag.). This system was started by the Greek astronomer Hipparchus in the second century BC. He divided the stars into six categories of brightness, from the brightest stars (first magnitude), to the faintest stars that he could see (sixth magnitude). Nowadays star brightnesses are measured to the nearest hundredth of a magnitude by sensitive instruments known as photometers. A difference of five magnitudes is now defined as being exactly equal to a brightness difference of 100 times; consequently, each magnitude step is equal to the 5th root of 100, which is approximately 2.5. The table (page 9) shows the difference in brightness that corresponds to a given magnitude difference. Stars over 2.5 times brighter than mag. 1 are given negative (minus) magnitudes, e.g. Sirius, the brightest star in the sky, which has a magnitude of −1.46. Stars fainter than 6th mag. are given progressively larger positive magnitudes. The faintest objects seen through telescopes on Earth have magnitudes of about 24. The constellation charts in this book are complete down to mag. 5.5; the total number of stars shown on them is approximately 3000. The sky atlas section of the book shows stars down to mag. 4.5.

The magnitude of diffuse objects such as star clusters, nebulae, galaxies and comets is more difficult to quantify than that of a star. A diffuse object's brightness is usually given as though all its light were concentrated into one star-like point.

Therefore a galaxy of 9th mag. appears of the same brightness as would an out-of-focus star of 9th mag., whose light was spread over the same area as the galaxy. The best way to estimate the brightness of diffuse objects is to compare them with the image of an out-of-focus star of known magnitude.

Conversion of magnitude difference into brightness difference

Difference in magnitude	Difference in brightness
0.5	1.6
1.0	2.5
1.5	4.0
2.0	6.3
2.5	10
3.0	16
3.5	25
4.0	40
5.0	100
6.0	250
7.5	1000
10	10,000
12.5	100,000
15	1,000,000

Star names

There are several different systems for identifying stars, as a result of which a given star may be referred to in more than one way. Many of the brightest stars have proper names, which are of Arabic, Greek and Latin origin; examples are Altair, Sirius and Regulus respectively. Another common system is to give the brightest stars in each constellation a Greek letter; this system was started in 1603 by the German celestial cartographer Johann Bayer, so that the Greek letters attached to stars are known as Bayer letters. For example, Sirius is also known as α (alpha) Canis Majoris, meaning that it is the star α (alpha) in the constellation Canis Major (note that the genitive form of the constellation's name is always used when referring to a star by its Bayer letter). Stars that are not identified in either of these ways may be given a number, called a Flamsteed number (e.g. 19 Lyncis), because they were introduced in a catalogue compiled by the first English Astronomer Royal John Flamsteed (1646–1719). Fainter stars are referred to by their numbers in any one of several star catalogues.

Greek alphabet

α	alpha	ι	iota	ϱ	rho
β	beta	κ	kappa	σ	sigma
γ	gamma	λ	lambda	τ	tau
δ	delta	μ	mu	υ	upsilon
ε	epsilon	ν	nu	φ	phi
ζ	zeta	ξ	xi	χ	chi
η	eta	ο	omicron	ψ	psi
θ	theta	π	pi	ω	omega

Various astronomers have also compiled specialized lists of particular types of stars, such as double stars, nearby stars, white dwarf stars, and these provide another source of nomenclature. In this book, some double stars catalogued by the Russian astronomer F. G. W. Struve are referred to by their

Struve numbers. Variable stars have a nomenclature all their own. Those that are not named under the existing systems are given one or two Roman letters (e.g. W Virginis, RR Lyrae). When all possible letter combinations have been used up, the variable stars in a constellation are denoted by the letter V and a number, e.g. V 1500 Cygni.

Objects such as star clusters, nebulae and galaxies have their own systems of nomenclature, the most familiar of which are the M and NGC numbers. The M numbers come from a catalogue of over 100 clusters and nebulous objects compiled in the eighteenth century by the French astronomer Charles Messier. The NGC numbers come from the *New General Catalogue of Nebulae and Clusters of Stars* published in 1888 by the Danish astronomer J. L. E. Dreyer. Two supplements to the NGC, called the *Index Catalogues*, appeared in 1895 and 1908; objects listed in these are given IC numbers. Some objects have both M numbers and NGC numbers.

Star types

Stars are incandescent balls of gas, similar in nature to the Sun but so far away that they appear as nothing more than points of light in even the largest telescopes. Nevertheless, by analysing the light from the stars, astronomers have been able to deduce that stars come in a wide range of sizes, temperatures, colours and brightnesses. The largest stars, aptly known as *giants* and *supergiants*, are hundreds of times the diameter of the Sun, so that they would encompass the orbit of the Earth if they were placed where our Sun is. Stars of such enormous girth are at a more advanced stage of evolution than our own Sun, which itself will swell up into a red giant towards the end of its life. Supergiants differ from ordinary giants simply by being more massive. At the other end of the scale are the *red dwarf* stars that have about one-tenth the diameter of the Sun; these are stars that were born with much less mass than the Sun. Most remarkable of all are the super-dense *white dwarf* stars which have the mass of the Sun packed into a sphere the size of the Earth. These are thought to be the exposed central cores of former red giant stars whose outer layers of rarefied gas have dissipated into space.

Star colours

Not all stars are white as they at first appear. More careful inspection reveals that stars come in a wide range of colours, from deep orange through yellow to blue-white. The colour of a star depends on its surface temperature, with the coolest stars being the reddest and the hottest ones the bluest. Therefore a star's colour is a clue to its physical nature. The stars with the most prominent colours are the red giants such as Betelgeuse in Orion, Aldebaran in Taurus and Antares in Scorpius. Star colours are more prominent through binoculars and telescopes than with the naked eye. Particularly attractive are double stars (p. 16) in which the stars are of contrasting colours.

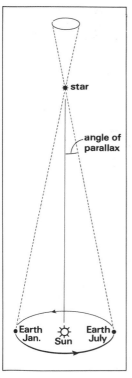

Star distances

Distances between stars and galaxies are usually measured either in light years (abbreviated l.y.) or parsecs: here the *light year* is used. It is the distance that a beam of light, moving at 300,000 km per second, travels in one year. One l.y. is equivalent to 9.5 million million km.

The distances of the nearest stars can be measured directly by a technique known as *parallax*. This involves measuring the star's precise position against the celestial background, as seen from opposite sides of the Earth's orbit. A shift in the star's position when seen from the two viewpoints (on either side of the Sun, six months apart) reveals the star's distance, with the nearest stars

Parallax, a star's change in position as seen from opposite sides of the Earth's orbit, reveals the star's distance.

to us showing the greatest amount of parallax shift. A star at a distance of 3.26 l.y. would show a parallax shift of one second of arc; hence a distance of 3.26 l.y. is known as a *parsec* (short for parallax of one second). In practice, no star is quite this close. The nearest star to us, α (alpha) Centauri, has a parallax of 0.76 seconds of arc, which makes its distance 4.3 l.y.

Beyond about 100 l.y. the parallaxes of stars are too small to be measured accurately by telescopes on the ground. Astronomers then have to use an indirect method that involves estimating the star's luminosity from features of its spectrum; they can then work out how far away from us the star must be to account for its brightness as seen in the sky. This method is open to considerable error, but it is the only technique we have for finding the distance of the majority of stars.

Variable stars

Some stars are not constant in brightness, but vary over periods of time ranging from hours to weeks or even years. The brightness of a variable star can be estimated by comparison with surrounding stars that do not vary in brightness.

The most common cause of variation is that the star actually pulsates in size as a result of an instability. A celebrated class of pulsating variables is the Cepheids, named after their prototype, δ (delta) Cephei. These are yellow supergiant stars that pulsate regularly every few days or weeks. Their importance to astronomers is that their period of pulsation is directly related to their luminosity, the brightest Cepheids taking the longest to pulsate. Consequently by observing a Cepheid's pulsation period, astronomers can accurately ascertain its luminosity, and by comparing the luminosity with the star's brightness as it appears from Earth, they can work out how far away it is. Cepheids are thus an important tool for calibrating distances in the Universe.

For all their importance, Cepheids are relatively rare. The most abundant type of variable stars are actually the red giants and supergiants, virtually all of which exhibit some form of variability due to pulsations in size, although they do not have the strict periodicity of Cepheids; a famous example of a red giant variable is *o* (omicron) Ceti, popularly known as Mira. Some red variable stars, such as the supergiant Betelgeuse, follow no detectable period at all.

A totally different type of variable star is the *eclipsing binary*. It consists of two stars in mutual orbit, one periodically moving in front of the other as seen from Earth. Each eclipse of one star by the other causes a dip in the total light that we receive. The most famous eclipsing binary star is Algol, also known as β (beta) Persei (see page 174).

Most spectacular of all are the eruptive variables which undergo sudden and often very large changes in light output, most notably the novae and supernovae. A *nova* is thought to be a close double star in which one member is a white dwarf. Gas from the companion star spills onto the white dwarf where it ignites explosively, causing the star's light to surge temporarily by thousands of times. The star is not destroyed in a nova explosion; some novae have been seen to erupt more than once, and possibly all novae may recur given time. Novae are often first spotted by amateur astronomers.

Even more spectacular than normal novae are the *supernovae*, celestial cataclysms that signal the death of a massive star. In a supernova, the star ends its life by blowing itself to bits, temporarily shining as brightly as billions of normal stars. Where the supernova occurred, the wreckage of the star is left to drift away into space, as with the Crab Nebula in Taurus and the Veil Nebula in Cygnus. To become a supernova, a star must have a mass several times that of our own Sun. The last supernova in our Galaxy was seen in 1604, and we are long overdue for another one.

Double and multiple stars

When examined through telescopes, many stars are found not to be single, as they appear to the naked eye, but to be accompanied by one or more companions. In some cases the stars are not really connected but simply happen to lie in the same line of sight by chance; such an arrangement is known as an *optical double*. But in the great majority of cases the stars are linked by gravity and orbit around each

16

Physical double star

Optical double star

other, the exact time taken depending on their distance apart. A pair of stars linked in this way is known as a *binary*; sometimes whole families of three or more stars, called *multiple stars*, may be interlinked by gravity.

The apparent separation of two stars in a double is measured in seconds of arc. (There are 60 seconds (″) in a minute (′) of arc, and 60 minutes of arc in a degree (°), so that one second of arc is 1/3600th of a degree. The apparent diameter of the Moon is about 30 minutes of arc, or half a degree.) The widest doubles – those with separations of several seconds of arc or more – can be divided in small telescopes or even binoculars, but the closer together the components of a double star are, the larger the aperture

In a physical double, two stars orbit each other; in an optical double, the stars lie in the same line of sight.

of telescope needed to separate them. The steadiness of the air, known as the seeing, will also affect the ability to separate close doubles. The best examples of observable doubles are described in the text accompanying each map.

Star clusters

Stars sometimes group together in clusters, of which there are two main types: open clusters and globular clusters. *Open clusters* are the less densely packed of the two types: they are usually irregular in shape, and contain anything up to many thousands of relatively young stars. They lie in the spiral arms of our Galaxy. Famous examples are the Pleiades and Hyades clusters in Taurus, and the Double Cluster in Perseus. Open clusters frequently cover half a degree of sky or more, i.e. are equal to or greater than the apparent diameter of the full Moon.

Globular clusters are dense, ball-shaped aggregations that can contain hundreds of thousands of stars. They are distributed in a halo around our Galaxy, so they are usually much further away from us than open clusters and in general they appear smaller and are more difficult to resolve into individual stars. In contrast to open clusters, globular clusters contain some of the oldest stars known. Famous examples are ω (omega) Centauri, 47 Tucanae, and M 13 in Hercules.

Nebulae

Nebulae are clouds of gas and dust in space, some of which glow brightly while others are dark. In bright nebulae, the gas and dust is lit up by the stars that lie within them. Famous examples of bright nebulae are the Orion Nebula and the Tarantula Nebula (in Dorado). By contrast, dark nebulae are visible only because they blot out light from objects behind them. One famous dark nebula is the Coalsack in Crux, the Southern Cross, which obscures part of the Milky Way star fields in that region. Some dark nebulae are seen in silhouette against bright nebulae.

Planetary nebulae

Planetary nebulae are clouds of gas that have been thrown off by a central star like the Sun at the end of its life. Their name is misleading, for planetary nebulae have nothing to do with real planets at all. Rather, the name was given because their appearance often resembles the disc of a planet, as seen through small telescopes.

Milky Way

All the stars visible to the naked eye are part of an enormous system of at least 100,000 million stars known as the Galaxy (our Galaxy is given a capital letter to distinguish it from other galaxies – see below). Those stars nearest to us in the Galaxy are scattered more or less at random across the sky and make up the constellations. The more distant ones mass into a faint band of light seen crossing the sky on clear nights. This is the Milky Way, and is shown on the constellation maps in this book as a light blue band. Sometimes the term Milky Way is used as an alternative name for our Galaxy. Our Galaxy has a spiral shape, with most of the stars and nebulae concentrated in curving arms that wind outwards from a bulging central core. The Galaxy is about 100,000 l.y. in diameter and the Sun lies 30,000 l.y. from its centre. The centre of our Galaxy lies in the direction of the constellation Sagittarius, a region in which the Milky Way star fields are particularly dense. The entire Galaxy is rotating; our Sun takes about 250 million years to complete one orbit around the centre of the Galaxy.

Galaxies

Galaxies extend into space as far as the largest telescopes can see. Each is a collection of millions or billions of stars held together by the mutual attraction of gravity. Galaxies are classified according to their shapes, of which there are two main forms: spiral and elliptical. Spiral galaxies are sub-divided into normal spirals and barred spirals. Our own Milky Way Galaxy is a normal spiral, as is the famous neighbour and near-twin of our own, the Andromeda Galaxy. Most galaxies within reach of amateur telescopes are also normal spirals, with a central bulge of stars from which arms curve outwards.

Above: a spiral galaxy, M 74 in Pisces. *Below:* a barred spiral galaxy, NGC 1300 in Eridanus. *Hale Observatories.*

Barred spirals differ by having a straight bar of stars across their centres; the spiral arms emerge from the ends of this bar. Spiral galaxies are oriented at different angles with respect to us, which affects the way they appear in the telescope. For instance, a spiral seen face-on appears circular in telescopes, but an edge-on spiral appears cigar-shaped.

Elliptical galaxies come in a wide range of sizes, from the most massive, to the smallest galaxies of all. They are elliptical in outline and have no spiral arms. There are also a few galaxies that are irregular in shape. These include the two Magellanic Clouds, which are satellite galaxies of our Milky Way, although there is a trace of spiral form in the Large Magellanic Cloud.

Since galaxies are faint and fuzzy, they are best viewed with low magnification to increase the contrast against the sky background.

Star positions and motions

In the sky, the equivalent of longitude and latitude is right ascension (R.A.) and declination (dec.). *Right ascension* starts at the place where the Sun on its yearly path around the sky (the ecliptic) moves northwards across the celestial equator. This point, known as the *vernal equinox*, is the celestial equivalent of the Greenwich meridian on Earth. Right ascension is measured eastwards from the vernal equinox around the sky in hours, from 0 to 24. Each hour of right ascension is divided into 60 minutes, and each minute is divided into 60 seconds. *Declination* is measured in degrees north and south of the celestial equator, from 0 degrees at the equator to +90 degrees at the north celestial pole and −90 degrees at the south celestial pole. The celestial poles lie directly above the Earth's poles, and the celestial equator is directly overhead as seen from the Earth's equator. The position of a star or any other object can therefore be specified precisely in terms of right ascension and declination, like the coordinates of a point on Earth. Coordinate grids are overlain on each of the star maps in this book.

But celestial cartographers are faced with two problems that do not concern their terrestrial counterparts. Firstly, each star is very slowly moving relative to its neighbours; and secondly, the entire coordinate grid is itself shifting due to a wobble of the Earth in space. The movements of the stars are known as their *proper motions*. With few exceptions, e.g. Barnard's Star (see page 162), the proper motions of stars are so small as to be undetectable over a human lifetime except by precise measurements. Over many thousands of years these motions will build up until the present shapes of the constellations are totally changed, and stars will have strayed into neighbouring constellations. One day, astronomers will have to revise the current nomenclature of stars and constellations.

The wobble of the Earth on its axis, called *precession*, causes the point where the ecliptic intersects the celestial equator to move once around the sky every 26,000 years. Therefore the coordinates of all points in the sky are gradually changing, and it is customary to give the coordinates of celestial objects with respect to a certain reference date. In the case of this book the reference date is the year 2000, so the star maps herein will be usable without serious error until the middle of the twenty-first century.

Planets

In addition to the fixed stars, the planets of our Solar System are also visible in the night sky. The planets shine by reflecting light from the Sun. Because they continually travel in orbit around the Sun, the planets are always moving, so they cannot be shown on the maps in this book. But when they do appear, the planets will be found near the ecliptic.

The brightest planet, Venus, outshines every star in the sky. It is frequently seen rising before the Sun in the morning sky, when it is popularly known as the morning star, or setting in the evening twilight when it is termed the evening star. A small telescope will reveal that Venus is not a star at all, for it shows a disk that goes through phases (like those of the Moon as it orbits the Sun). The second-brightest planet is Jupiter, which at its brightest can also easily outshine any star. Unlike Venus, which keeps close to the Sun, Jupiter can be seen in any part of the sky. Even binoculars, if held steadily, reveal its four brightest moons that circle it incessantly (Io, Europa,

Ganymede, Callisto), changing their positions from night to night.

Mars and Saturn can also feature prominently in the night sky. Mars is notable because of its glaring red colour, but it is a disappointing sight in amateur telescopes because of its small size. Saturn, by contrast, is perhaps the most beautiful telescopic sight of all, being encircled by a halo of rings composed of snowballs that orbit it like a swarm of tiny moons. Of the other planets, Mercury is an elusive object, never straying far enough from the Sun to be easily visible, and Uranus, Neptune and Pluto are distant and faint.

Meteors

Occasionally a bright streak of light will be seen darting across the sky, lasting no more than a second or so. This is a *meteor*, popularly known as a *shooting star*. Meteors have nothing to do with stars. They are actually specks of dust burning up by friction as they dash at high speed into the Earth's upper atmosphere. We do not see the speck of dust itself, but rather the trail of hot gas that it produces as it burns up at a height of about 100 km.

On any clear night a few meteors can be seen without binoculars each hour; these random arrivals are known as *sporadic meteors*. But several times each year the Earth passes through a swarm of interplanetary dust, which gives rise to a *meteor shower*. The members of a meteor shower all appear to come from one small area of sky, known as the *radiant*. The shower is named after the constellation in which the radiant lies, e.g. the Geminids appear to radiate from Gemini. One exception is the Quadrantids, which radiate from a part of the sky once occupied by the now-defunct constellation Quadrans Muralis, the mural quadrant, now part of Boötes. A meteor shower may last for days or even weeks as the Earth passes through the swarm of dust, but usually the peak of activity is confined to one particular night.

In the case of the richest showers, such as the Perseids in August, dozens of meteors per hour can be seen. Sometimes the meteors explode along their path, becoming bright enough to cast shadows. Some meteors leave trains which slowly fade. The number of meteors in a shower is expressed in terms of the *zenithal hourly rate* (ZHR). This is the number of meteors an observer would see each hour if the radiant were directly overhead: in practice it seldom is, and so the actual number of meteors seen will be less than the ZHR. Also, if conditions are less than perfect – e.g. polluted skies or the presence of bright Moonlight – then the number of meteors seen will again be reduced. The main meteor showers of the year are listed in the table opposite.

Annual meteor showers

Shower	Date(s) of maximum	ZHR
Quadrantids	3–4 January	100
Lyrids	21–22 April	12
η (eta) Aquarids	5–6 May	40
δ (delta) Aquarids	28–29 July	20
Perseids	12 August	60
Orionids	21 October	20
Taurids	3 November	12
Leonids	17–18 November	10
Geminids	13–14 December	60

Key to the symbols used on the constellation maps.

V

CENTAURUS

CRUX
Mimosa
Acrux

MUSCA

APUS

PAVO

GRUS

TUCANA

PHOENIX

12ʰ

CHAMAELEON

OCTANS

HYDRUS

10ʰ

VELA

8ʰ

CARINA

PUPPIS

Canopus

VOLANS

MENSA

PICTOR

COLUMBA

6ʰ

DORADO

RETICULUM

CAELUM

HOROLOGIUM

4ʰ

Achernar

ERIDANUS

2ʰ

0ʰ

−90°
−80°
−70°
−60°
−50°
−40°

Variable stars

ANDROMEDA

A large constellation of the northern hemisphere of the sky that represents the daughter of Queen Cassiopeia and King Cepheus. In Greek mythology, Andromeda was chained to a rock as a sacrifice to the sea monster Cetus, but was saved from certain death by the intervention of the hero Perseus.

Bright star

α (alpha) Andromedae (Sirrah or Alpheratz) is a blue-white star of mag. 2.1. Its two alternative names both come from the Arabic meaning 'horse's navel', for it was once considered to be part of neighbouring Pegasus. It now marks the head of Andromeda.

Double stars

γ (gamma) Andromedae is a glorious double star. Even small telescopes easily divide its two components of mags. 2.2 and 5.0. Their beautifully contrasting colours of yellow and blue make this one of the showpiece doubles of the sky.

56 And is a pair of 6th-mag. yellow giant stars, divisible in binoculars, near to the star cluster NGC 752.

Star cluster

NGC 752 is a large, scattered binocular cluster of up to 100 stars of 9th and 10th-mag.

continued

ANDROMEDA

Galaxies

M 31 (NGC 224), the great Andromeda Galaxy, one of the most famous objects in the entire sky, is the most distant object visible to the naked eye. It is a spiral galaxy similar to our own Milky Way, lying 2.2 million l.y. away. On clear, dark nights it can be seen by the naked eye as a hazy smudge; binoculars show its elliptical shape more distinctly. Only the brightest central part of the galaxy is visible through amateur instruments. Long-exposure photographs reveal the full extent of its spiral arms, which span nearly 3° of sky, i.e. six times the width of the full Moon. Also visible in small amateur telescopes is a satellite galaxy, known as M 32 or NGC 221, which appears like a fuzzy 9th-mag. star 0.5° south of M 31's core. Another satellite galaxy, NGC 205, is larger but fainter, and lies over 1° northwest of M 31.

Planetary nebula

NGC 7662 is one of the easiest planetary nebulae to see with small amateur telescopes. Under high magnification it appears as a fuzzy blue-green disc with an elliptical outline.

The Andromeda Galaxy, M 31, with its companions M 32
(below centre) and NGC 205 (upper right). *Hale Observatories*.

ANTLIA The Air Pump

A faint and obscure constellation in the southern hemisphere of the sky, representing the pump invented by the English physicist Robert Boyle. There are no bright stars in Antlia.

Double star

ζ^1 ζ^2 (zeta^1 zeta^2) Antliae is a wide pair of 6th-mag. stars easily seen in binoculars. Small telescopes show that ζ^1 (zeta^1) Ant also has a 7th-mag. companion.

Planetary nebula

NGC 3132 on the borders with Vela is a large, bright planetary nebula of similar size to the more famous Ring Nebula in Lyra but a full magnitude brighter. In telescopes it appears as a hazy, elliptical disc larger than the apparent size of the planet Jupiter.

APUS The Bird of Paradise

An unremarkable constellation in the south polar region of the sky. It contains no bright stars.

Double star

δ^1 δ^2 (delta^1 delta^2) Apodis is a pair of 5th-mag. orange giant stars easily visible in binoculars.

ANTLIA

-20°
11h
10h
9h
CRATER
HYDRA
-30°
θ
α
ζ² ζ¹
PYXIS
η
ε
ι
CENTAURUS
-40°
U
3132
PUP
VELA
2

APUS

60°
ARA
TRIANGULUM
AUSTRALE
CIRCINUS
Rigil Kentaurus
Hadar
CENTAURUS
ζ
-70°
18h
16h
κ¹
14h
ι
MUSCA
PAVO
R
θ
β
δ²
α
12h
20h
γ
δ¹
ε
η
-80°
OCTANS
CHAMAELEON
3

AQUARIUS The Water Carrier

A constellation of the zodiac, through which the Sun passes from mid February to mid March. Aquarius represents a man pouring water from a jar.

Double star
ζ (zeta) Aquarii is the central star of the Y-shaped grouping that makes up the water jar of Aquarius. It is a tight pair of 4th-mag. white stars, which need telescopes of at least 75mm aperture and high magnification to be divided.

Globular clusters
M 2 (NGC 7089) is a rich globular cluster of 6th mag. It appears as a hazy patch in binoculars and small telescopes.

M 72 (NGC 6981) is a 9th-mag. globular cluster, unimpressive in small telescopes.

Planetary nebulae
NGC 7009, the Saturn Nebula, appears as a small greenish disk of 8th mag. in small telescopes. It is named the Saturn Nebula because in large telescopes its shape resembles that of the planet Saturn.

NGC 7293, the Helix Nebula, is the closest planetary nebula to us, about 600 l.y. away, and the largest in apparent size. Its diameter is 16′ of arc, half that of the Moon. Although large it is faint, and is best seen
continued

AQUARIUS

DELPHINUS

+10°   0°   AQUILA   −10°   −20°

                                                                3   μ Albali   CAPRICORNUS
                                                                         ε
                                                                         M72
                                                                         ⊕
EQUULEUS   Sadalsuud   7009   ν
                                                                    M73   21ʰ

                        ⊕ M2   β
                                               ξ   ECLIPTIC

PEGASUS   22ʰ
                π Sadalmelik   ρ ϑ
                ζ α   ι
                η   γ   ν 7293   PISCES AUSTRINUS
                   Sadachbia   σ
                      κ

                         λ   τ² δ Skat
                                                                              86   23ʰ
                                               τ¹   88

                      φ   98
                       χ
                       ψ² ψ¹   99
                        ψ³
                         ω² ω¹

PISCES

                                                                                    SCULPTOR

CET   0ʰ
                                                                                    4

AQUILA The Eagle

A constellation straddling the celestial equator, representing an eagle.

Bright star

α (alpha) Aquilae (Altair, Arabic for flying eagle) is a white star of mag. 0.8. It forms one corner of the so-called Summer Triangle of stars, the other two being Deneb in Cygnus and Vega in Lyra. Altair is 16 l.y. away, one of the closest stars to us.

Variable star

η (eta) Aquilae is one of the brightest Cepheid variables, ranging from mag. 4.1 to mag. 5.3 every 7.2 days. *continued*

Aquarius continued

in binoculars, or telescopes with low magnification, which show it as a circular misty patch. Its full beauty is brought out in long-exposure photographs, where it appears like two overlapping loops of gas.

Meteors

Three meteor showers radiate from Aquarius each year. The richest shower, the η (eta) Aquarids, reach a maximum of about 40 per hour on 5 May; the δ (delta) Aquarids produce about 20 meteors per hour around 28 July; and on 6 August the ι (iota) Aquarids reach about 8 meteors per hour.

AQUILA

VULPECULA

LYRA

SAGITTA

HERCULES

ϱ

φ   γ   χ
o   Tarazed
Altair
ξ   α
β   Alshain
σ

ζ   ε
ω¹

6709

+20°

+10°

DELPHINUS

OPH

μ

δ

SERPENS
CAUDA

η

ν

θ

71

ι

AQR

15   14
λ
12

κ

0°

−10°

57

SAGITTARIUS

SCUTUM

CAPRICORNUS

20ʰ

19ʰ

5

ARA The Altar

A small constellation of the southern celestial hemisphere, visualized by the Greeks as the altar on which Centaurus the centaur was about to sacrifice Lupus the wolf. It has no stars brighter than 3rd mag.

Star cluster
NGC 6193 is a binocular cluster of about 30 stars, the brightest of which is of 6th mag.

Globular cluster
NGC 6397 is possibly the closest globular cluster to us, about 7500 l.y. away. It appears as a 7th-mag. smudge in binoculars and small telescopes.

Aquila continued

Double stars
15 Aquilae is a 5th-mag. yellow star with a 7th mag. companion easily visible in small telescopes.

57 Aquilae is an easy pair of 6th-mag. stars for small telescopes.

SAGITTARIUS

SCORPIUS

CORONA
AUSTRALIS

-40°

LUPUS

σ
ι
⊕ 6352
○ 6193

λ
α

-50°

ϑ

μ
κ

6397 ⊕

π

β

ε²
ε¹

TELESCOPIUM

γ

ζ

η

NORMA

δ

-60°

PAVO

⊕ 6362

TRIANGULUM
AUSTRALE

CIR

-70°

18ʰ

17ʰ

16ʰ

15ʰ

19ʰ

20ʰ

OCTANS

APUS

6

ARIES The Ram

An important constellation of the zodiac; the Sun is in Aries from late April to mid March. Aries represents the ram whose golden fleece was sought by Jason and the Argonauts. The importance of Aries lies in the fact that it once contained the vernal equinox, i.e. the point where the Sun crosses the celestial equator moving from south to north; this is the zero point of right ascension, the celestial equivalent of the Greenwich meridian. The effect of precession has now moved the vernal equinox into neighbouring Pisces, but for historical reasons the vernal equinox is still referred to as the First Point of Aries.

Bright star
α (alpha) Arietis (Hamal, from the Arabic for sheep), is a yellow giant of mag. 2.0.

Double stars
γ (gamma) Arietis is an easy pair for small telescopes, consisting of two white stars of 5th mag.

λ (lambda) Arietis is a 5th-mag. white star with a 7th-mag. companion visible in binoculars or small telescopes.

π (pi) Arietis, a blue-white 5th-mag. star, has a close 8th-mag. companion visible in small telescopes under high magnification.

ARIES

PISCES

ANDROMEDA

1ʰ

+30°

+20°

2ʰ

TRIANGULUM

Sheratan
β
Mesarthim
γ
ι
λ
α
κ
η
Hamal

ν

ECLIPTIC

ξ

+10°

PERSEUS

3ʰ

41

ε

π

σ

CETUS

ζ
δ

τ

Pleiades

TAURUS

4ʰ

7

AURIGA The Charioteer

A large constellation of the northern hemisphere of
the sky. γ (gamma) Aurigae is shared with Taurus,
and is dealt with under that constellation as β (beta)
Tauri.

Bright star
α (alpha) Aurigae (Capella), mag. 0.1, is the 6th-
brightest star in the entire sky. It is a yellow giant
42 l.y. away.

Variable star
ε (epsilon) Aurigae is an eclipsing binary of excep-
tionally long period. Every 27 years it sinks from
mag. 3.0 to 3.8 as it is eclipsed by a dark companion;
the eclipses last for a full year. Its last eclipse was in
1983.

Double stars
θ (theta) Aurigae is a tight double of mag. 2.6 with a
7th-mag. companion requiring at least 100 mm
aperture and high magnification to distinguish.

ω (omega) Aurigae is a double star for small telescopes consisting of stars of 5th and 8th mags.

Star clusters
M 36 (NGC 1960) is a binocular cluster of 60 stars.

continued

AURIGA

BOÖTES The Herdsman

A large constellation of the northern celestial hemisphere, representing a man driving the bear of Ursa Major around the sky.

Bright star

α (alpha) Boötis (Arcturus, from the Greek for bear-keeper), mag. 0.0, is the 4th-brightest star in the entire sky. It is a red giant 36 l.y. away.

Double stars

ε (epsilon) Boötis (Izar or Pulcherrima) is a glorious but difficult pair with contrasting colours of orange and blue, of 3rd and 5th mag. Their closeness requires at least 75mm aperture and high power to split.

μ (mu) Boötis, a blue-white star of 4th mag., has a 7th-mag. binocular companion. The companion is itself double, as revealed under high power by telescopes of at least 75mm aperture.

continued

Auriga continued

M 37 (NGC 2099) is the richest of the clusters in Auriga. It contains about 150 stars.

M 38 (NGC 1912) is a large, scattered binocular cluster of about 100 stars. Next to it lies NGC 1907, a much smaller and fainter cluster.

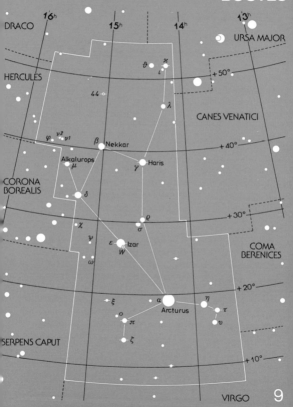

BOÖTES

DRACO

16ʰ   15ʰ   14ʰ   13ʰ

URSA MAJOR

HERCULES

+50°

ϑ ϰ
  ι

λ

CANES VENATICI

φ ν2 ν1
       β Nekkar

+40°

Alkalurops
     μ   γ Haris

CORONA
BOREALIS

δ

+30°

χ
ν   ϱ
      σ

ω   ε Izar
         W

COMA
BERENICES

+20°
ξ   α   η τ
o   Arcturus   υ
π
     ζ

SERPENS CAPUT

+10°

VIRGO   9

CAELUM The Chisel

A faint and easily overlooked constellation of the southern sky. Its brightest star is of mag. 4.5.

Double star

γ (gamma) Caeli is a pair of 5th and 8th mag. stars for small telescopes.

Boötes continued

ν¹ ν² (nu¹ nu²) Boötis are a wide pair of unrelated white and orange 5th-mag. stars.

ξ (xi) Boötis is a beautiful duo for small telescopes, consisting of a yellow and an orange star of 5th and 7th mags.

Meteors

The Quadrantids, the year's most abundant meteor shower, radiate from the northern part of Boötes, reaching a maximum of about 100 meteors per hour on 3–4 January. The shower takes its name from a now-abandoned constellation, Quadrans Muralis, the Mural Quadrant, that once occupied this area of sky. Although they are plentiful, the Quadrantids are not as bright as other great showers such as the Perseids.

CAELUM

LEPUS

−20°

ERIDANUS

COLUMBA

−30°

γ

FORNAX

β

−40°

α

δ

PUPPIS

−50°

HOROLOGIUM

Canopus

CARINA

PICTOR

6ʰ

5ʰ

DORADO

4ʰ

3ʰ

RETICULUM

10

CAMELOPARDALIS The Giraffe

A large but inconspicuous constellation in the north polar region of the sky, which also used to be called Camelopardus. Its brightest stars are of 4th mag.

Double stars

β (beta) Camelopardalis is a yellow supergiant of mag. 4.0, the brightest star in the constellation; it has a wide 9th-mag. companion visible in small telescopes and good binoculars.

Struve 1694 (Σ 1694) is an attractive pair of 5th and 6th mag. white stars easily split in small telescopes.

Star cluster

NGC 1502 is a small binocular cluster of about 15 stars. Small telescopes reveal two easy double stars at its centre, one pair of 6th mag. and the other pair of 9th mag.

Galaxy

NGC 2403 is a 9th-mag. spiral galaxy visible in binoculars under good conditions.

CAMELOPARDALIS

URSA MINOR

DRACO

DRACO

URSA MAJOR

Σ1694

+90° Polaris

CEPHEUS

VZ

2403

CASSIOPEIA

γ

LYNX

α

β

1502

AURIGA

PERSEUS

11

CANCER The Crab

A constellation of the zodiac, inside whose boundaries the Sun lies from late July to early August. The constellation represents the crab that attacked Hercules during his fight with Hydra, the water snake. In times past, the Sun used to lie in Cancer when at its farthest north of the celestial equator; this is the time of the summer solstice, 21 June each year. The latitude at which the Sun appears overhead when farthest north came to be known as the Tropic of Cancer. However, because of the effect of precession, the Sun now lies in neighbouring Gemini on the summer solstice.

Double stars

ζ (zeta) Cancri is an attractive pair of yellow stars of 5th and 6th mags. visible through small telescopes.

ι (iota) Cancri is a 4th-mag. yellow giant with a 7th-mag. companion easily seen with small telescopes.

Star cluster

M 44 (NGC 2632), Praesepe, also popularly termed the Beehive Cluster, is a large swarm of 75 or more stars of 6th mag. and fainter. To the naked eye it appears as a misty patch. It is best seen in binoculars because of its great size, covering 1.5° of sky, three times the apparent width of the full Moon.

CANCER

AUR

10h +40°

LEO MINOR

LYNX

9h

8h

Castor

σ2
RS
σ3
+30°
τ

ϱ2 ι

χ

Pollux

GEMINI

ν

γ Asellus Borealis
η
μ
+20°
Praesepe
M44
δ
ϑ
ζ

LEO

Asellus Australis

ECLIPTIC

π

ο¹

BP

Acubens
M67
α
+10°
κ

β

Procyon

CANIS MINOR

0°

HYDRA

MONOCEROS 12

CANES VENATICI The Hunting Dogs

A constellation of the northern hemisphere of the sky, representing the two dogs of Boötes, the herdsman.

Double star

α (alpha) Canum Venaticorum is known as Cor Caroli, meaning Charles's Heart, a name given by Edmond Halley in honour of Charles II of England. It is a blue-white star of mag. 2.9 with a 5th-mag. companion easily seen in small telescopes.

Globular cluster

M 3 (NGC 5272), of 6th mag., is visible as a hazy patch in binoculars. Although telescopes of 100mm are needed to resolve individual stars, smaller telescopes show it as a softly glowing ball of light.

Galaxies

M 51 (NGC 5194) is the famous Whirlpool Galaxy, a spiral with a satellite galaxy, NGC 5195, at the end of one of its arms. Large telescopes are needed to show it to effect; in small telescopes it appears as a hazy patch with starlike points marking the nuclei of the main galaxy and its satellite.

M 94 (NGC 4736) is an 8th-mag. spiral galaxy seen face on, looking like a small comet in amateur telescopes.

CANES VENATICI

15ʰ

DRACO

14ʰ

13ʰ

12ʰ

+ 60°

11ʰ

URSA MAJOR

BOÖTES

+ 50°

M51

M106

γ

4449

M63

M94

β

Asterion

α Cor Caroli

+ 40°

4631

+ 30°

LEO

M3

COMA BERENICES

+ 20°

13

CANIS MAJOR The Greater Dog

A compact constellation in the southern hemisphere of the sky, containing many bright stars, notably Sirius, the brightest star of all. It represents one of the dogs of Orion, the other being represented by Canis Minor.

Bright stars

α (alpha) Canis Majoris (Sirius, from the Greek for sparkling or scorching) is the brightest star in the entire sky, of mag. −1.5. It is a white star 8.7 l.y. away, one of the closest stars to the Sun. It has an 8th-mag. white dwarf companion visible only in large amateur telescopes.

β (beta) Canis Majoris (Mirzam, the announcer, i.e. of Sirius) is a blue giant of mag. 2.0.

δ (delta) Canis Majoris (Wezen) is a yellow supergiant of mag. 1.9, 3000 l.y. away.

ε (epsilon) Canis Majoris (Adhara, the virgins), mag. 1.5, is a blue giant with an 8th-mag. companion, difficult to see in small telescopes because of the glare from the main star.

Star cluster

M 41 (NGC 2287) is a large, bright cluster whose brightest star is of 7th mag. It is just visible to the naked eye and is well seen in binoculars and small

continued

CANIS MAJOR

CANIS MINOR

ORION

MONOCEROS

0°

−10°

FR

ϑ
μ
γ
ι
α Sirius
β
ν³
ν² Mirzam
π
M41

LEPUS

−20°

ξ² ξ¹

o²
UW τ
2362
EW
ω δ
Wezen
σ
ε Adhara
Aludra
η
ζ

o¹

−30°

κ λ

PUPPIS

COLUMBA

−40°

8ʰ
7ʰ
6ʰ

PICTOR 14

CANIS MINOR The Lesser Dog

A small constellation lying on the celestial equator. It represents the smaller of the two dogs of Orion, Canis Major being the larger. Apart from Procyon, its brightest star, it contains little of interest. Procyon forms a triangle of brilliant stars with Sirius (in Canis Major) and Betelgeuse (in Orion).

Bright star

α (alpha) Canis Minoris (Procyon, from the Greek meaning before the dog, i.e. it rises before Canis Major), mag. 0.4, is the 8th-brightest star in the sky. It is a yellow-white star 11.3 l.y. away, one of the nearest stars to the Sun.

Canis Major continued

telescopes. Its brightest stars seem to be arranged in chains.

NGC 2362 is a cluster of about 40 stars for binoculars or small telescopes, surrounding the 4th-mag. blue giant τ (tau) Canis Majoris.

CANIS MINOR

GEMINI

CANCER

Pollux

ECLIPTIC

+20°

+10°

γ ε
Gomeisa β
η
Procyon α

ζ δ¹

0°

HYDRA

MONOCEROS

−10°

CANIS MAJOR

PUPPIS

8ʰ 7ʰ Sirius

15

CAPRICORNUS The Sea Goat

A constellation of the zodiac, through which the Sun passes from late January to mid-February. It represents a goat with a fish tail. In ancient times the Sun lay in Capricornus at the winter solstice, its farthest point south of the equator. The effect of precession has now moved the winter solstice into neighbouring Sagittarius, but the latitude on Earth at which the Sun appears overhead on that day is still known as the Tropic of Capricorn.

Double stars

α (alpha) Capricorni (Algedi, from the Arabic meaning goat or ibex) is a naked-eye pair of unrelated 4th-mag. stars. Each star is itself double. Small telescopes show that α^1 (alpha^1) Capricorni has a 9th-mag. companion, and α^2 (alpha^2) Capricorni has an 11th-mag. companion.

β (beta) Capricorni is a 3rd-mag. star with a 6th mag. companion for binoculars or small telescopes.

Globular cluster

M 30 (NGC 7099) is an 8th-mag. globular cluster next to the 5th-mag. star, 41 Capricorni.

CAPRICORNUS

AQUILA

SAGITTARIUS

ECLIPTIC

MICROSCOPIUM

AQUARIUS

PISCIS AUSTRINUS

α²α¹ Algedi
ν
β Dabih
σ
π
ρ
τ
υ
ψ
ω
θ
η
χ
φ
24
ζ
ι
κ
ε
41 ⊕ M30
λ
μ
γ
Deneb Algedi
δ
Nashira

20ʰ

21ʰ

22ʰ

−10°
−20°
−30°

16

CARINA The Keel

A large constellation of the southern celestial hemisphere. Carina is one of the parts into which the constellation of Argo Navis, the ship of the Argonauts, was divided. It lies in an area of the Milky Way rich with clusters and nebulae.

Bright stars

α (alpha) Carinae (Canopus), mag. −0.7, is the second-brightest star in the sky. It is a yellow-white supergiant 1200 l.y. away.

β (beta) Carinae (Miaplacidus) is a blue-white star of mag. 1.7.

ε (epsilon) Carinae is a yellow giant star of mag. 1.9.

Variable star

η (eta) Carinae is one of the most erratically behaved stars in the heavens. In 1843 it flared up to a maximum of mag. −1, but has now settled to around 6th or 7th mag. It lies inside the nebula NGC 3372 (see page 73). η (eta) Carinae is thought to be an unstable supergiant star with a mass of over 100 Suns that throws off shells of gas at irregular intervals. It is expected to become a supernova in the next 10,000 years.

continued

CARINA

PUPPIS

RET

HYDRUS

PICTOR

DORADO

MENSA

CHAMAELEON

VELA

Miaplacidus

MUSCA

CEN

CRU

Canopus

α
A
N
χ

2516

ε
f
d
c
g
a
j
h
R
2808

3114
I2581
s
u
S
p
q
θ
I2602
3372
T
3293
v
3532
x

β
G
I

ω

17

Carina continued

Double star

υ (upsilon) Carinae is a 3rd-mag. white star with a 6th-mag. companion visible in small telescopes.

Star clusters

IC 2602 is a large and bright cluster similar to the Pleiades, centred on the 3rd-mag. blue-white star θ (theta) Carinae. It contains six naked-eye stars, and many more are visible in binoculars and small telescopes covering over 1° of sky.

NGC 2516 is a large binocular cluster of about 100 stars, containing a 5th-mag. red giant and three double stars of 8th and 9th mags. for small telescopes.

NGC 3532 is a large binocular cluster of 150 stars of 6th mag. and fainter, very rich in small telescopes which show its markedly elliptical shape. A 4th-mag. orange star at one edge is apparently not a member of the cluster, but is much more distant.

Nebula

NGC 3372, the η (eta) Carinae Nebula, is a diffuse nebula visible to the naked eye, larger than the Orion Nebula. It is bisected by a dark V-shaped lane of dust. NGC 3372 contains the erratic variable star η (eta) Carinae, which lies in the bright central part of the nebula near to a dark notch called the Keyhole because of its shape. This is a star-studded region for sweeping with binoculars (see opposite).

CASSIOPEIA

A distinctive W-shaped constellation of the northern hemisphere of the sky, representing a mythical Queen of Ethiopia, wife of King Cepheus and mother of Andromeda.

Variable star

γ (gamma) Cassiopeiae is an unstable blue giant that throws off shells of gas at irregular intervals, causing it to vary unpredictably between 2nd and 3rd mags.

Double and multiple stars

η (eta) Cassiopeiae is a beautiful double star for small telescopes consisting of yellow and red components of 4th and 8th mags.

ι (iota) Cassiopeiae is a 5th-mag. white star with an 8th-mag. companion divisible in small telescopes. The brighter star has a close 7th-mag. yellow companion visible with 100mm aperture and high magnification.

Star clusters

M 52 (NGC 7654) is a binocular cluster of over 100 stars, somewhat kidney-shaped and with a prominent 8th-mag. orange star at one edge.

NGC 457 is an attractive cluster for small telescopes, including the 5th-mag. yellow supergiant φ (phi) Cassiopeiae. The stars of NGC 457 are seemingly arranged in chains.

CASSIOPEIA

18

CENTAURUS The Centaur

A resplendent constellation of the southern celestial hemisphere, representing the mythical beast known as a centaur. It contains the closest known star to the Sun, α (alpha) Centauri, which is actually a triple system.

Bright stars

α (alpha) Centauri (Rigil Kentaurus, from the Arabic meaning foot of the centaur) appears to the naked eye as a star of mag. −0.3, the third-brightest in the sky. Small telescopes split it into a pair of yellow stars of mags. 0.0 and 1.4 which orbit each other every 80 years. These two stars lie 4.3 l.y. away from us. About 0.1 l.y. closer is an 11th-mag. red dwarf called Proxima Centauri; this is strictly the closest star of all to us. Proxima Centauri lies 2° away in the sky from its two brighter companions, not even in the same telescopic field of view.

β (beta) Centauri (Hadar or Agena) is a blue giant of mag. 0.6, the 11th-brightest star in the sky. A line drawn from α (alpha) through β (beta) Centauri points to Crux, the Southern Cross.

Double star

3 Centauri (also known as k Centauri) is a neat pair of blue-white stars of 5th and 6th mags. for small telescopes.

continued

CENTAURUS

19

Planetary nebula

NGC 3918 is an 8th-mag. planetary nebula with a
small blue-green disk similar in appearance to the
planet Uranus. John Herschel called this the Blue
Planetary.

Globular cluster

ω (omega) Centauri (NGC 5139) is the largest and
brightest globular cluster in the sky, covering a
larger area than the full Moon. To the naked eye it
appears as a fuzzy 4th-mag. star, somewhat elliptical
in outline. Small telescopes or even binoculars begin
to resolve its outer regions into a granular mass of
sparkling stars. It is one of the closest globulars to
us, about 16,000 l.y. away.

Galaxy

NGC 5128 is a peculiar galaxy also known as the radio
source Centaurus A, visible in binoculars or small
telescopes as a 7th-mag. hazy blur. Long-exposure
photographs show that it is a giant elliptical galaxy
crossed by a band of dark dust. One possibility is
that we are seeing an elliptical galaxy merging with
a spiral galaxy, the spiral galaxy providing the lane
of dust. It is one of the strongest sources known to
radio astronomers, who have detected lobes of radio
emission either side of the galaxy, as though it has
ejected clouds of gas in a series of explosions. It lies
about 15 million l.y. away.

The enormous radio galaxy NGC 5128, also known as Centaurus A, can be seen in small telescopes. *Hale Observatories.*

79

CEPHEUS

A constellation of the north polar region of the sky, representing a mythical King of Ethiopia, husband of Queen Cassiopeia and father of Andromeda. It contains the celebrated variable star δ (delta) Cephei.

Variable stars

δ (delta) Cephei is the prototype of the most important type of variable stars known to astronomers, the Cepheid variables. Thanks to the so-called Period-Luminosity Law, astronomers can derive a Cepheid's absolute magnitude by observing its period of variation; Cepheid variables are therefore the 'standard candles' by which astronomers measure distances in space. The variability of δ (delta) Cephei was discovered in 1784 by the English amateur astronomer John Goodricke. δ (delta) Cephei is a yellow supergiant that varies between mags. 3.6 and 4.3 every 5 days 9 hours. δ (delta) Cephei is also a double star (see following page).

μ (mu) Cephei is a red supergiant, prototype of the class of semiregular variables. It varies between mags. 3.6 and 5.1 with no set period. Sir William Herschel named it the Garnet Star on account of its pronounced coloration: it is one of the reddest stars visible to the naked eye.

continued

CAMELOPARDALIS

URSA MINOR

+90°
Polaris

16ʰ

4ʰ

2ʰ

18ʰ

+80°

0ʰ

22ʰ

20ʰ

Er Rai

γ

ϱ

χ

DRACO

π

+70°

Alfirk

β

τ

ο

ι

 θ

ξ

VV

Alderamin

7160

α

η

+60°

ν

λ

CASSIOPEIA

δ

ζ

μ

ε

I 1396

+50°

LACERTA

CYGNUS

ANDROMEDA

20

Double stars

β (beta) Cephei is a blue giant of 3rd mag. with an 8th-mag. companion visible in small telescopes. β (beta) Cephei is also a variable star, though its fluctuations are too small to be noticed with the naked eye, less than 0.1 mag. every 4.5 hours. It is the prototype of a class of pulsating variable stars (also known as β (beta) Canis Majoris stars) with periods of a few hours and small changes in light output.

δ (delta) Cephei, in addition to being a noted variable star (see page 80 and comparison chart opposite), is an attractive double star for small telescopes or even binoculars. The brighter cream-coloured component, which is the variable, is accompanied by a wide 6th-mag. blue-white star.

ξ (xi) Cephei is a double star for small telescopes consisting of a blue-white star of 5th mag. with a 7th-mag. yellowish companion.

ο (omicron) Cephei is a 5th-mag. yellow giant with a close 7th-mag. companion visible in apertures of 60mm and above with high magnification.

δ Cephei

CETUS The Whale

A large constellation straddling the celestial equator, representing the sea monster that nearly devoured Andromeda before her rescue by Perseus.

Nearby star
τ (tau) Ceti is a 3rd-mag. yellow dwarf, 11.7 l.y. away. Of all the nearby single stars, this one is most similar to our own Sun.

Variable star
o (omicron) Ceti (Mira, the wonderful), a red giant, is the prototype of the long-period variables. Mira fluctuates between 3rd and 9th mags. with an average period of 330 days. Its variability was first noticed in 1596 by the Dutch astronomer David Fabricius.

Double stars
α (alpha) Ceti (Menkar, from the Arabic for nose) is a red giant of 2nd mag. with an unrelated blue 6th-mag. companion visible in binoculars.

γ (gamma) Ceti (Kaffaljidhmah) is a close pair of 4th and 6th-mag. stars requiring at least 60mm aperture and high power to split.

continued

PEG

+10°   0°   AQR   -10°   -20°

0ʰ

PISCES

ECLIPTIC

ι

SCULPTOR

7

φ1

φ2   246

Deneb Kaitos

β   247   T

φ3

η

1ʰ

θ

τ

χ

ζ

ν

2ʰ

AR

ξ1

ξ2

ν   Kaffaljidhma

γ   ο Mira

δ

ρ

σ

μ

M77

ε   π

FORNAX

λ

α

κ   Menkar

TAU

ERIDANUS

3ʰ

ARIES

21

CHAMAELEON The Chameleon

An insignificant constellation in the south polar region of the sky, representing a chameleon. Its brightest stars are of 4th mag.

Double star
δ (delta) Chamaeleontis is a binocular pair of blue and orange stars of 4th and 5th mags. They are unrelated, lying in the same line of sight by chance.

Planetary nebula
NGC 3195 is a planetary nebula of similar apparent size to the planet Jupiter.

Cetus continued

Galaxy
M 77 (NGC 1068) is a 9th-mag. spiral galaxy presented face on. It is unimpressive in small telescopes, but its main interest is that it is the brightest of the so-called Seyfert galaxies, spiral galaxies with bright centres that are closely related to quasars.

CHAMAELEON

CRUX CENTAURUS VELA

Mimosa

−60°

Acrux

CEN

CARINA

−70°

VOLANS

CIR

MUSCA

12h

10h

8h

14°

−80°

κ

ε

γ

ν

α

β

δ¹

η ϑ

δ²

ι

ζ

3195

16°

−90°

APUS

MENSA

ζ

18h

4

OCTANS

0h

20h

22h

0h

HYDRUS

PAVO

22

CIRCINUS The Compasses

A small and obscure constellation of the southern hemisphere of the sky, overshadowed by neighbouring Centaurus.

Double star

α (alpha) Circini is a 3rd-mag. white star with a wide 9th-mag. companion visible in small telescopes.

COLUMBA The Dove

A constellation of the southern hemisphere of the sky, usually envisaged as a dove following along after Noah's Ark. It contains no objects of interest to amateur observers.

Runaway star

μ (mu) Columbae, a 5th-mag. blue star, is one of three so-called runaway stars that seem to be diverging from a point in Orion at speeds of around 100 km/sec. The other two stars are 53 Arietis and AE Aurigae. According to one theory the stars were once members of a quadruple system, the fourth member of which exploded as a supernova about three million years ago.

CIRCINUS

LUPUS

16ʰ 15ʰ 14ʰ 13ʰ

NORMA

CENTAURUS

β

γ

Hadar

δ ϑ

Rigil
Kentaurus

ε η

α

60°

Mimosa

CRUX

Acrux

TRIANGULUM
AUSTRALE

APUS

MUSCA

70°

23

COLUMBA

LEPUS

CANIS MAJOR

ERIDANUS

Adhara

ν²

30°

σ μ

λ

δ γ α

κ β ε ο

ϑ ξ

π² η

1851

40°

PUPPIS

7ʰ 6ʰ 5ʰ

CAELUM

HOR

24

COMA BERENICES Berenice's Hair

A faint constellation of the northern sky, representing the locks of the Egyptian Queen Berenice which
she offered to the gods for the return of her husband
from battle. Coma Berenices contains a number of
galaxies within range of amateur telescopes; these
are members of the Virgo Cluster that have spilled
over the border.

Double star
24 Comae Berenicis, a 5th-mag. orange giant, makes
a beautiful colour contrast with a 7th-mag. blue-
white companion, visible in small telescopes.

Star cluster
The Coma Star Cluster consists of a scattered group
of about 30 stars representing Queen Berenice's
severed tresses. They form a V-shaped binocular
group to the south of γ (gamma) Comae Berenicis.
The brightest members are of 5th and 6th mag.

Globular cluster
M 53 (NGC 5024) is an 8th-mag. globular cluster,
visible as a misty patch in small telescopes.

Galaxy
M 64 (NGC 4826) is a 9th-mag. spiral galaxy visible
in small telescopes. It is popularly called the Black
Eye Galaxy because of a dark patch of dust near its
centre, shown by telescopes of 150mm and above.

URSA
MAJOR

CANES VENATICI

LEO

β

North
Galactic Pole

γ

4565

FZ

M64

BOÖTES

M53

α
Diadem

24

M85

M100

M98

M91

M88

M99

VIRGO

ECLIPTIC

14ʰ

13ʰ

12ʰ

+ 40°

+ 30°

+ 20°

+ 10°

0°

25

CORONA AUSTRALIS
The Southern Crown

A small constellation of the southern hemisphere of the sky, lying between Sagittarius and Scorpius. Corona Australis has been known since Greek times, and is said in legends to represent the crown worn by the neighbouring centaur, Sagittarius. Despite its small size it is not without interest, lying on the edge of the Milky Way.

Double stars

γ (gamma) Coronae Australis is a tight pair of 5th-mag. yellow stars requiring at least 100mm aperture and high magnification to split.

κ (kappa) Coronae Australis is a wide pair of 6th-mag. blue-white stars easily divided by small telescopes.

λ (lambda) Coronae Australis is a 5th-mag. white star with a wide 9th-mag. companion easily seen in small telescopes.

Globular cluster
NGC 6541 is a 6th-mag. globular cluster, 14,000 l.y. away, for binoculars and small telescopes.

CORONA AUSTRALIS

SER

ECLIPTIC

−20°

−30°

OPHIUCHUS

SAGITTARIUS

SCORPIUS

γ
α
ε
λ
κ
β
δ
μ
ϑ
ζ
η²
η¹
6541

−40°

ARA

−50°

TELESCOPIUM

−60°

ND

PAVO

20ʰ

19ʰ

18ʰ

17ʰ

26

CORONA BOREALIS
The Northern Crown

A small constellation of the northern hemisphere of the sky. Its most distinctive feature is a crescent-shaped group of stars in which the constellation's brightest star, mag. 2.2 Gemma (also known as Alphecca), is set like a jewel in the crown.

Variable stars
R Coronae Borealis is a celebrated variable star given to catastrophic changes in brightness at intervals of a few years. Normally it is of 6th mag. but it can unpredictably drop in a few weeks to as low as 14th mag., subsequently taking some months to return to its former brightness. Its variation is thought to be due to sooty carbon particles in its outer layers, which periodically build up and then blow away.

T Coronae Borealis, known as the Blaze Star, is a recurrent nova that normally hovers around 10th mag. but which in 1866 and 1946 brightened to 2nd and 3rd mags. respectively. Further eruptions may be expected at any time.

Double stars
ζ (zeta) Coronae Borealis is a pair of 5th and 6th-mag. blue stars for small telescopes.

$v^1 v^2$ (nu^1 nu^2) Coronae Borealis is a wide binocular pair of unrelated 5th-mag. orange giants.

CORVUS The Crow

A small constellation of the southern hemisphere of the sky. In Greek legends, Corvus is linked with Crater and Hydra. The crow (Corvus) is sent on an errand to fetch water in a cup (Crater), but returns with the water snake (Hydra) instead.

Double star

δ (delta) Corvi is an unequal double for small telescopes, consisting of a 3rd-mag. white star accompanied by a wide 8th-mag. companion.

CRATER The Cup

An insignificant constellation representing the goblet of Apollo. Its brightest stars are of 4th mag., and there are no objects of interest for amateur observers.

ANTLIA

SEXTANS

LEO

HYDRA

α

β

ξ

ε

γ

λ

θ

ι

ξ

η

CRATER

11ʰ

12ʰ

ε

γ

ξ

Al Chiba α

CORVUS

δ

η

β

VIRGO

ECLIPTIC

CENTAURUS

13ʰ

30°

20°

10°

0°

Spica

CRUX The Southern Cross

The smallest constellation in the sky, but one of the most famous and distinctive. It lies in a rich region of the Milky Way, on the borders of Centaurus.

Bright stars

α (alpha) Crucis (Acrux) is of mag. 0.9 to the naked eye, and is the 14th-brightest star in the sky. But small telescopes split it into two sparkling blue-white components of mags. 1.4 and 1.9.

β (beta) Crucis (Mimosa) is a blue-white star of mag. 1.3.

Double star

μ (mu) Crucis is an easy pair of blue-white stars of 4th and 5th mags. for small telescopes.

Star cluster

NGC is a showpiece cluster known as the Jewel Box because of its glittering appearance in telescopes. Its brightest star is the 6th-mag. blue supergiant κ (kappa) Crucis; the whole cluster is sometimes termed the κ (kappa) Crucis cluster.

Nebula

The Coalsack is a dark cloud of dust that blots out the bright star background of the Milky Way. The whole of the Coalsack measures $7° \times 5°$, and extends into neighbouring Centaurus and Musca.

CRUX

40°

CENTAURUS

−50°

−60°

μ γ
λ Mimosa
β   δ
κ   4755   ε
ι
        Acrux β2
        α   η   θ1
        ζ

13ʰ   12ʰ

14ʰ   −70°

11ʰ

RCINUS

5ʰ
λA

CARINA

MUSCA

10ʰ

APUS

CHAMAELEON

30

CYGNUS The Swan

A prominent constellation of the northern skies, sometimes known as the Northern Cross because of its cruciform shape. Cygnus represents a swan flying along the Milky Way. In one legend Cygnus is the Greek god Zeus in disguise; another identifies the swan with Orpheus. The Milky Way is particularly rich in the region of Cygnus.

Bright star
α (alpha) Cygni (Deneb, from the Arabic meaning tail) is a blue-white supergiant star of mag. 1.3.

Variable stars
χ (chi) Cygni is a red giant long-period variable which reaches its brightest, 4th or 5th mag., every 407 days. At its faintest it sinks to 12th mag.

P Cygni is a blue supergiant of 5th mag. which has flared up to 3rd mag. in the past, apparently as a result of throwing off shells of gas.

Double stars
β (beta) Cygni (Albireo) is a beautiful coloured double star, one of the showpieces of the sky. It consists of a yellow giant of 3rd mag. accompanied by a 5th-mag. blue-green star visible in small telescopes or even good binoculars. Not to be missed by any observer.

continued

HERCULES
HER
DRACO
LYRA
Vega
+30°
18ʰ
+40°
+50°
19ʰ
+60°
Albireo
β
φ
ι
ϑ
χ
η
π²
6826
δ
CEPHEUS
ψ
20ʰ
26
σ²
σ¹
ο²
ο¹
ρ
M29
39
41
33
ω²
ω¹
α
Deneb
γ
Sadr
λ
ε
Gienah
52
VULPECULA
21ʰ
ν
T
6960
CASSIOPEIA
ξ
7000
61
σ
τ
υ
6992
ζ
π¹
22ʰ
π²
W ϱ
M39
75
μ
LACERTA
23ʰ
ANDROMEDA
PEGASUS

o^1 (omicron^1) Cygni is a 4th-mag. orange giant that forms an attractive wide binocular duo with the 5th-mag. blue giant 30 Cygni. Closer to o^1 (omicron^1) Cygni is a 7th-mag. blue companion visible in binoculars or small telescopes. o^1 (omicron^1) Cygni is an eclipsing binary with a very long period of nearly 10.5 years, which varies by only a few tenths of a mag.

61 Cygni is a famous pair of orange dwarf stars of 5th and 6th mags., easily split in small telescopes. They lie 11.1 l.y. away, and are among the closest neighbours to the Sun.

Planetary nebula
NGC 6826 is known as the Blinking Planetary Nebula, because it seems to blink on and off as one looks alternately at it and away from it. Telescopes of 75mm aperture show its 8th-mag. pale blue disk. The nebula lies within 1° of the 6th-mag. 16 Cygni, an easy double star for small telescopes.

Nebulae
NGC 6992 is the brightest part of the loop that makes up the Veil Nebula; it can only be seen in wide-angle telescopes with low power, or under the very best conditions with binoculars. The Veil Nebula itself is the remains of a supernova that ex-

ploded over 50,000 years ago, and consists of a number of faint streamers in a loop-shape – most of it is only seen well on long-exposure photographs.

The Cygnus Rift, also known as the Northern Coalsack, is a dark lane of dust that divides the bright Milky Way in this region, as can be seen by the naked eye on clear nights.

NGC 7000 is a large patch of bright nebulosity known as the North America Nebula because of its shape. Despite its size it is a difficult object for amateur observers, because of its low surface brightness, but it can be seen in binoculars on clear dark nights.

Black hole
Although by definition invisible, the object known as Cygnus X-1 is thought to be the first black hole ever identified. Its existence is known because it is an X-ray source. It lies near to the star η (eta) Cygni.

Radio galaxy
Cygnus A, near γ (gamma) Cygni, is one of the strongest radio sources known to astronomers. It is a radio galaxy of 18th mag., far beyond the reach of all but large professional telescopes. Long-exposure photographs show Cygnus A as a pair of fuzzy blobs in contact; this is either a galaxy undergoing an explosion or two galaxies in collision.

DELPHINUS The Dolphin

A small constellation in the equatorial region of
the sky with a distinctive kite-shape. It represents
a dolphin, one of the messengers of the sea-god
Poseidon. Although not bright, its four main stars
form a box-shaped group known as Job's Coffin.
The peculiar names of two of these stars, Sualocin
and Rotanev, first appeared in a star catalogue published at Palermo Observatory, Italy, in 1814. Read
backwards, they give Nicolaus Venator, which is the
Latinized form of Niccolo Cacciatore, the observatory's assistant director at that time. Delphinus
lies on the edge of the Milky Way in an area noted for
novae.

Double stars

γ (gamma) Delphini is a noted double star consisting
of golden and yellow-white stars of 4th and 5th mag.,
divisible in small telescopes. Struve 2725, a fainter
and closer double of 7th and 8th mags., lies nearby
in the same field of view.

DELPHINUS

CYGNUS

21ʰ   20ʰ

+30°

VULPECULA

+20°

SAGITTA

γ   α Sualocin
δ   β Rotanev
      ζ
       η
       ε

PEGASUS

+10°   Altair

κ

EQUULEUS

0°

AQUARIUS   AQUILA

-10°

CAPRICORNUS   CAPRICORNUS   32

DORADO The Goldfish

A constellation of the southern sky, sometimes also known as the Swordfish. Its main feature is the Large Magellanic Cloud, the larger and more distant of the two satellite galaxies that accompany our Milky Way.

Variable star
β (beta) Doradus is one of the brightest Cepheids, varying from mags. 3.8 to 4.7 every 9 days 20 hours.

Galaxy
The Large Magellanic Cloud is an irregularly-shaped galaxy about 180,000 l.y. away, containing perhaps 10,000 million stars (less than ten percent of the number in our own Galaxy). It is visible to the naked eye as a hazy patch 6° across, like a detached portion of the Milky Way. Binoculars and small telescopes show that it is richly studded with bright stars, clusters and nebulae.

Nebula
NGC 2070 is a glowing cloud of hydrogen gas in the Large Magellanic Cloud. It is popularly known as the Tarantula Nebula because of its spidery shape, and is visible to the naked eye as a fuzzy star. At the centre of the Tarantula is a cluster of supergiant stars, which includes some of the most massive stars known. Were it as close as the Orion Nebula it would fill the entire constellation of Orion and cast shadows.

DRACO The Dragon

An extensive constellation of the northern polar region. It represents a dragon, lying with one of the feet of Hercules firmly planted upon its head.

Double and multiple stars

v (nu) Draconis is an outstanding binocular pair of 5th-mag. white stars.

o (omicron) Draconis is a 5th-mag. yellow giant with an 8th-mag. blue companion visible in small telescopes.

ψ (psi) Draconis is a pair of 5th and 6th-mag. yellow stars divisible in small telescopes or even binoculars.

16-17 Draconis is a binocular pair of 5th-mag. blue-white stars. Telescopes show a 7th-mag. companion closer to one of the stars, making a striking triple system.

39 Draconis is another impressive triple system. Binoculars show it as a wide pair of yellow and blue 5th and 7th-mag. stars, but telescopes reveal an 8th-mag. companion closer to the brighter star.

40-41 Draconis is an easy pair of 6th-mag. yellow stars for small telescopes.

continued

EQUULEUS The Little Horse

The second-smallest constellation, lying in the equatorial region of the sky. It is sometimes also called the Foal or Colt, and one legend identifies it as Celeris, the brother of neighbouring Pegasus. Its brightest star is of 4th mag.

Double and multiple stars

γ (gamma) Equulei (Kitalpha, little horse) is a 5th-mag. white star with a 6th-mag. binocular companion.

ε (epsilon) Equulei is a 5th-mag. yellow star with a blue-white 7th-mag. companion visible in small telescopes. The brighter (yellow) star is itself double, requiring apertures of 150mm to split it into two close 6th-mag. stars; these orbit each other every 101 years.

Draco continued

Planetary nebula

NGC 6543 is one of the most prominent planetary nebulae, appearing as an irregularly shaped blue-green disk (like an out-of-focus star) in amateur telescopes.

EQUULEUS

CYGNUS

VULPECULA

22ʰ

21ʰ

+30°

+20°

PEGASUS

+10°

δ γ

β

α
Kitalpha

ε

DELPHINUS

SAGITTA

0°

AQUARIUS

AQUILA

< 10°

ECLIPTIC

CAPRICORNUS

35

ERIDANUS The River

An extensive constellation, 6th-largest in the sky, that meanders from the celestial equator far into the southern celestial hemisphere. In Greek legends, Eridanus represents the river into which Phaethon fell after his attempt to drive the chariot of his father the Sun God, but it has also been identified with real rivers such as the Po of Italy, the Nile and the Euphrates. Despite its size Eridanus has few bright stars. It contains a number of distant galaxies which are too faint for amateur telescopes, but which show up well on long-exposure photographs.

Bright star
α (alpha) Eridani (Achernar, from the Arabic meaning end of the river) is a blue-white star of mag. 0.5, the 9th-brightest star in the entire sky.

Nearby star
ε (epsilon) Eridani, mag. 3.7, is a yellow dwarf similar to the Sun, lying 10.7 l.y. away.

Double and multiple stars
θ (theta) Eridani is an impressive pair of 3rd and 4th-mag. blue-white stars for small telescopes.

o^2 (omicron²) Eridani (also called 40 Eridani) is a remarkable triple star containing the most easily
continued

ERIDANUS

ORION
TAURUS
0°

μ ν ξ 32
Mira

β
Gursa
ψ ω o¹
o² δ ε ξ θ¹ o²
CETUS

λ
Rigel π η
10°
S 1535
53
γ πCet

LEPUS
54
20°
τ⁵ τ⁴
τ⁹ τ⁶ τ³ τ²
τ⁷ τ¹
τ⁸

30°
υ¹
υ²
υ⁴
υ³
9
FORNAX
f

COLUMBA CAELUM
Acamar
40°
e ϑ ι SCL
s
PHOENIX
κ
HOROLOGIUM

50°
φ χ

PICTOR
Achernar
α
5ʰ 4ʰ 3ʰ 2ʰ 60°
DORADO RETICULUM HYI
36

FORNAX The Furnace

A barren constellation of the southern hemisphere of the sky, originally known as Fornax Chemica (the chemical furnace). It contains a number of faint galaxies, beyond the reach of all but large amateur telescopes, which are its main interest.

Double star

α (alpha) Fornacis is a 4th-mag. yellow star with a close 6th-mag. companion, possibly variable, visible through moderate-sized amateur telescopes.

Eridanus continued

observable white dwarf in the sky. The 4th-mag. main star is a Sun-like yellow dwarf. Small telescopes show a 10th-mag. companion; this is the white dwarf. Telescopes of 100mm aperture reveal an 11th mag. third member of the system. This is a red dwarf, completing a rare trio that is not to be missed.

32 Eridani, 220 l.y. away, is a beautiful coloured double for small telescopes, consisting of 5th and 6th-mag. stars of yellow and blue-green.

Planetary nebula

NGC 1535 is a 9th-mag. planetary nebula visible as a blueish disk in small telescopes.

FORNAX

-10°

ERIDANUS

CETUS

-20°

ϰ

γ² *ω*

α *ν*

-30°

μ *π*

δ *β*

φ

SCL

η³

-40°

ERIDANUS

PHOENIX

HOROLOGIUM

DORADO

4ʰ -50°

3ʰ

2ʰ

37

GEMINI The Twins

Gemini is a major zodiacal figure, the Sun passing through the constellation from late June to late July.

Bright stars

α (alpha) Geminorum (Castor) appears of mag. 1.6 to the naked eye. Telescopes of at least 60mm aperture and high magnification split Castor into two blue-white stars of 2nd and 3rd mag. Also visible is a wider 9th-mag. red dwarf. These three stars are spectroscopic binaries, so Castor actually consists of six stars.

β (beta) Geminorum (Pollux) is an orange giant, mag. 1.1.

Variable stars

ζ (zeta) Geminorum is a 4th-mag. Cepheid variable that fluctuates by about 0.4 mag. every 10.2 days.

η (eta) Geminorum is a red giant semi-regular variable. It fluctuates from 3rd to 4th mag. about every 230 days.

Double stars

ε (epsilon) Geminorum is a 3rd-mag. yellow supergiant with a wide 9th-mag. companion visible in small telescopes.

38 Geminorum is an attractive white and yellow pair of 5th and 8th-mag. stars, for small telescopes.

continued

GEMINI

TAURUS

ORION

Betelgeuse

AURIGA

6ʰ

M35

η

μ

ν

γ

30

λ⁴⁵

38

MONOCEROS

ϑ

S

7ʰ

ε

+40°

τ

α

ξ

δ

λ

BQ

ρ

ι

2392

Castor

υ

κ

ECLIPTIC

σ

β

π

φ

χ

8ʰ

CANIS MINOR

Pollux

LYNX

+30°

CANCER

+20°

+10°

38

GRUS The Crane

A constellation of the southern hemisphere of the sky, representing a water bird, the crane.

Double stars

δ (delta) Gruis is a naked-eye double of 4th-mag. stars.

μ (mu) Gruis is a naked-eye double of 5th-mag. stars.

Gemini continued

Star cluster

M 35 (NGC 2168) is an outstanding cluster of over 100 stars, visible as a misty patch in binoculars; telescopes resolve it into curving chains of stars.

Planetary nebula

NGC 2392 is shown by small telescopes as an 8th-mag. blue-green disk about the size of Jupiter. It is popularly known as the Eskimo or Clown Face Nebula because of its appearance through large telescopes.

Meteors

The Geminid meteors, one of the year's most prominent showers, radiate from near Castor around 13–14 December each year. At maximum as many as 60 meteors per hour can be seen, many of them bright and explosive.

GRUS

AQUARIUS

CAPRICORNUS

SCULPTOR

PISCIS AUSTRINUS

Fomalhaut

30°

MIC

40°

ψ

λ

γ

ϱ

ω
μ²
μ¹

ξ

ϑ

δ¹
δ²

ι

Alnair

β

α

PHOENIX

50°

ε

ζ

η

κ

INDUS

60°

23ʰ

22ʰ

21ʰ

0ʰ

TUCANA

PAVO

39

HERCULES

A northern hemisphere constellation, and the 5th-largest in the sky. In Greek legends, Hercules was the son of Zeus who was set 12 labours in punishment for killing his wife and children in a fit of madness. A group of four stars makes up a shape known as the Keystone, which marks the pelvis of Hercules; on one side of the Keystone lies the celebrated globular cluster M 13, one of the finest objects of its kind.

Variable star

α (alpha) Herculis (Ras Algethi, from the Arabic meaning the kneeler's head) is a red supergiant that varies erratically between 3rd and 4th mag. Small telescopes show that it is also a double star, with a 5th-mag. blue-green companion.

Double stars

ϱ (rho) Herculis is a pair of 4th and 5th-mag. blue white stars divisible in small telescopes.

κ (kappa) Herculis is a 5th-mag. yellow giant with a 6th-mag. companion, easily seen in small telescopes.

95 Herculis is an attractive pair of 5th-mag. stars for small telescopes, appearing gold and silver.

continued

0ʰ

19ʰ 18ʰ DRACO 17ʰ 16ʰ 15ʰ

+60°

+50°

CYGNUS

BOÖTES

LYRA

τ υ
φ
σ g χ

ι M92 ⊕

+40°

Vega

ϑ ϱ π η

M13 ⊕ CORONA BOREALIS

+30°

u

ε ζ

ν

o ξ μ λ

δ

6210 β

JL +20°

110
109
102 95

γ
κ

111

ω

Ras Algethi α

+10°

AQUILA

OPHIUCHUS

SERPENS
CAPUT

SERPENS
CAUDA

40

HOROLOGIUM The Pendulum Clock

A faint and barren constellation of the southern skies, containing scarcely any objects of note. Its brightest star is of 4th mag.

Variable stars

R Horologii is a red giant long-period variable that fluctuates over a wide range, 5th to 14th mag. approximately every 400 days.

TW Horologii is a deep-red semi-regular variable that fluctuates between 5th and 6th mags.

Hercules continued

Globular clusters

M 13 (NGC 6205) contains 300,000 stars, and is the brightest globular cluster in the northern skies, a showpiece for all apertures. It is visible to the naked eye as a 6th-mag. misty patch on clear nights, and is prominent in binoculars. Small telescopes begin to resolve the cluster into stars, giving it the appearance of a mottled mound of sparkling stardust. M 13 lies about 22,500 l.y. away.

M 92 (NGC 6341) is a smaller and somewhat fainter cluster than M 13, but readily visible in binoculars. It is more condensed at the centre than M 13.

-30°

FORNAX

-40°

δ

α

CAELUM

PHOENIX

ERIDANUS

R

-50°

ι

η

PICTOR

ζ

TW

RETICULUM

μ

λ

Achernar

-60°

ν

β

DORADO

TUCANA

-70°

4ʰ   3ʰ   2ʰ   1ʰ

5ʰ

6ʰ

MENSA

HYDRUS

HYDRA The Water Snake

The largest constellation in the sky, yet it is far from prominent. Its most readily recognizable feature is a group of stars that make up its head, lying just north of the celestial equator. From there its tail snakes away to the southwest, towards Centaurus and Lupus; the total length of the constellation is over 100°. In Greek mythology, Hydra was the multi-headed monster slain by Hercules as one of his 12 labours. In another legend it is linked with the story of the crow, Corvus, who was sent to fetch water in a cup, represented by the constellation Crater. The constellations of Corvus and Crater are found on Hydra's back.

Bright star

α (alpha) Hydrae (Alphard, from the Arabic meaning solitary one) is an orange giant of mag. 2.0. It is the only star in the entire constellation that is brighter than mag. 3.0.

Variable stars

R Hydrae is a red giant long-period variable similar to Mira in Cetus. It fluctuates between 4th and 10th mags. every 386 days.

U Hydrae is a deep-red irregular variable star, that fluctuates between 5th and 6th mags. with no set period.

Double stars

ε (epsilon) Hydrae is a challenging double star, consisting of yellow and blue components, of 3rd and 7th mag., that require at least 75mm aperture to be separated.

27 Hydrae is a 5th-mag. yellow giant with a very wide 7th-mag. binocular companion. Small telescopes reveal that this star itself has a 9th-mag. companion.

54 Hydrae is a 5th-mag. yellow giant with a 7th-mag. purple companion for small telescopes.

I Hydrae is a 5th-mag. blue-white star with a wide 8th-mag. companion visible in small telescopes or good binoculars.

Star cluster

M 48 (NGC 2548) is a large binocular cluster of about 80 stars of 9th mag. and fainter, arranged in a triangular shape. Small telescopes resolve the brightest of its individual stars.

Planetary nebula

NGC 3242 is a 9th-mag. planetary nebula for small telescopes. It appears as a hazy blue-green disk known as the Ghost of Jupiter because of its similarity to the telescopic appearance of that planet.

continued on p. 128

HYDRA

LEO

ECLIPTIC

Regulus

CANCER

SEXTANS

ε
ω ζ ρ δ
ϑ η σ

τ²
τ¹

α Alphard
27

C
M48

CRATER

U
λ
υ²
υ¹ κ
ν φ μ
3242

12

MON

χ¹

I

ξ

ANTLIA

PYXIS

PUPPIS

11ʰ

10ʰ

9ʰ

8ʰ

VELA

42

HYDRUS The Lesser Water Snake

An insignificant constellation of the south polar region of the sky. Its brightest stars are of 3rd mag.

Double star

π (pi) Hydri is a wide binocular or naked-eye pair of unrelated 5th-mag. red and orange stars.

Hydra continued

Globular cluster

M 68 (NGC 4590) is a small, 8th-mag. globular cluster, unspectacular in small instruments; apertures of 150mm are needed to resolve its individual stars.

Galaxy

M 83 (NGC 5236) is an impressive 8th-mag. spiral galaxy seen face-on, and is one of the brightest of its kind in the southern sky. Through small telescopes it appears as a misty patch with a bright nucleus; apertures of 150mm are needed to trace its spiral arms.

HYDRUS

ERIDANUS

HOROLOGIUM

PHOENIX

Achernar

RETICULUM

α

TUCANA

DORADO

ζ

π² π¹ η²

ε

δ

ϑ

κ

γ

ν

h

μ 2ʰ β

INDUS

MENSA

4ʰ

0ʰ

VOL

δ

22ʰ

CHAMAELEON

OCTANS

20ʰ

-50°

-60°

-70°

-80°

-90°

43

INDUS The Indian

A faint constellation of the southern hemisphere of the sky. It represents a North American native Indian.

Nearby star
ε (epsilon) Indi is a yellow dwarf star similar to the Sun, 11.2 l.y. away, appearing of mag. 4.7.

Double star
θ (theta) Indi is a pair of 5th and 7th-mag. stars that can be separated by small telescopes.

LACERTA The Lizard

A very inconspicuous constellation of the northern hemisphere of the sky, sandwiched between Andromeda and Cygnus. Its brightest stars are of 4th mag. Lacerta lies in the Milky Way and has been the site of three bright novae this century, but it contains no objects of note for users of small telescopes.

LEO The Lion

A constellation of the zodiac, through which the Sun passes from mid-August to mid-September. It represents the lion slain by Hercules as part of his 12 labours.

Bright star
α (alpha) Leonis (Regulus, the little king) is a blue-white star of mag. 1.4. Binoculars and small telescopes show a wide 8th-mag. companion.

Variable star
R Leonis is a red giant long-period variable that fluctuates between 5th and 10th mags. with an average period of about 310 days.

Double and multiple stars
γ (gamma) Leonis (Algieba, Lion's mane) is a show-piece pair of yellow giants of 2nd and 3rd mags. divisible in small telescopes. In binoculars an un-related 5th-mag. star, 40 Leonis, is seen nearby.

ζ (zeta) Leonis is an optical triple star of 3rd mag. In binoculars ζ (zeta) Leonis appears to have two companions of 6th mag. at different distances from it, but both are unrelated to it.

τ (tau) Leonis is a 5th-mag. orange giant with a 7th-mag. binocular companion.

continued

LEO

LEO MINOR The Lesser Lion

A faint and obscure constellation of northern skies, sandwiched between Ursa Major and Leo. It contains no objects for users of small instruments.

Leo continued

Galaxies

Leo contains a number of interesting galaxies, none particularly easy for small telescopes. M 65 (NGC 3623) and M 66 (NGC 3627) are a pair of spiral galaxies of 9th and 8th mag. respectively; M 66 is presented at an angle to us and appears cigar-shaped. M 95 (NGC 3351) and M 96 (NGC 3368) are two more spiral galaxies, of 10th and 9th mags. All these objects require low power and a dark night to be picked out as faint smudges.

Meteors

The yearly Leonid meteor shower appears around 17 November, radiating from a point near γ (gamma) Leonis. Usually the numbers are low, peaking at about 10 per hour, but occasionally tremendous storms of up to 100,000 meteors per hour have been seen. These storms occur when the Earth passes near to the parent comet, Tempel-Tuttle, which has an orbital period of 33 years. The last such storm was in 1966; another spectacular Leonid meteor storm may occur in 1999.

12ʰ

+50°

11ʰ

10ʰ

9ʰ

URSA MAJOR

+40°

β

46

21

10

LYNX

CANCER

+30°

+20°

LEO

ECLIPTIC

Regulus

+10°

LEPUS The Hare

A constellation of the southern hemisphere of the sky. Although overshadowed by neighbouring Orion and Canis Major it is not without interest for amateur observers.

Variable star
R Leporis is a deep-red long-period variable, known as Hind's Crimson Star. It varies from 6th to 10th mags. about every 430 days.

Double star
γ (gamma) Leporis is an attractive binocular duo of yellow and orange stars, of 4th and 6th mags.

Star cluster
NGC 2017 is a star cluster that is really a multiple star. Binoculars and small telescopes show a group of five stars of 6th to 10th mag. Two of these stars are themselves close doubles, as revealed by apertures of 150mm, making this a group of at least seven related stars.

Globular cluster
M 79 (NGC 1904) is a compact 8th-mag. globular cluster for small telescopes. It lies near a 5th-mag. triple star, Herschel 3752, also visible in small telescopes.

TAU

0°

ORION

MONOCEROS

ә

-10°

Rigel

η
ϑ   ζ   ν ι
                       λ   κ
SS   R
Sirius   2017   α   μ
              Arneb

-20°   ERIDANUS

δ   β
γ   ε

M79 ⊕

CANIS MAJOR

-30°

PUPPIS   COLUMBA   CAELUM

-40°   6ʰ   5ʰ

48

LIBRA The Scales

A faint constellation of the zodiac through which the Sun passes during November. It is now seen as the scales of Astraea, goddess of justice, but once represented the claws of neighbouring Scorpius.

Variable star

δ (delta) Librae is an eclipsing binary of the same type as Algol. It varies between mags. 4.8 and 5.9 every 2 days 8 hours.

Double and multiple stars

α (alpha) Librae (Zubenelgenubi, from the Arabic meaning southern claw) is a 3rd-mag. blue-white star with a wide 5th-mag. companion easily visible in binoculars.

ι (iota) Librae is a complex multiple star. To the naked eye it appears of 4th mag. Binoculars show a wide 6th-mag. companion, 25 Librae. In small telescopes another, fainter companion is visible; apertures of 75 mm show that this companion actually consists of a close pair of 10th-mag. stars.

μ (mu) Librae is a 6th-mag. star with a close 7th-mag. companion for telescopes of 75mm aperture.

Globular cluster

NGC 5897 is a 10th-mag. globular cluster with loosely scattered stars, unspectacular in small instruments.

LIBRA

HER

16ʰ

SERPENS CAPUT

15ʰ

VIRGO

0°

16

OPHIUCHUS

Zubeneschamali β   δ

10°

ε   ξ²

μ

48   ECLIPTIC

γ Zubenelakrab   ν   α² α¹

η   Zubenelgenubi

θ   ζ

λ κ

5897 ⊕   20°

σ

Antares

ν   HYDRA

τ

30°

SCORPIUS   LUPUS   CENTAURUS

49

LUPUS The Wolf

A constellation of the southern sky, depicted as a wolf held in the grasp of neighbouring Centaurus.

Double and multiple stars

ε (epsilon) Lupi is a 3rd-mag. blue-white star with a 9th-mag. companion for small telescopes.

η (eta) Lupi is a 3rd-mag. blue-white star with an 8th-mag. companion, not easy to see in the smallest telescopes because of the brightness difference.

κ (kappa) Lupi is an easy pair of 4th and 6th-mag. stars for small telescopes.

μ (mu) Lupi is a 4th-mag. star with a 7th-mag. companion visible in small telescopes. Telescopes of at least 100mm aperture show that this companion is itself a tight pair of 5th-mag. stars.

ξ (xi) Lupi is a neat pair of 5th and 6th-mag. stars for small telescopes.

π (pi) Lupi consists of a close pair of 5th-mag. stars, divisible with apertures of 75mm and above.

Star cluster

NGC 5822 is a large cluster of at least 100 faint stars for binoculars and small telescopes.

ECLIPTIC

20°

VIR

OPH

LIBRA

Antares

HYDRA

2

30°

SCORPIUS

χ

ξ ψ¹

ψ²

φ¹

CENTAURUS

θ

⊕ 5986

φ²

η

υ

GG

γ

δ

40°

ω

β

o

ε

λ

τ¹

π

τ²

ι

υ¹

μ

κ

α

ϱ

σ

ζ

50°

NORMA

5822

CIRCINUS

ARA

16ʰ

15ʰ

14ʰ

60°

17ʰ

TRIANGULUM
AUSTRALE

Rigil
Kentaurus

Hadar

50

LYNX The Lynx

An exceedingly faint constellation of northern skies, named (by the Polish astronomer Johannes Hevelius) because only the lynx-eyed would be able to see it. Changes of constellation boundaries have produced confusion in the stellar nomenclature of this region. For instance, Lynx contains the star 10 Ursae Majoris, while the star known as 41 Lyncis lies in Ursa Major.

Double and multiple stars

5 Lyncis is a 5th-mag. orange giant with an 8th-mag. companion visible in small telescopes.

12 Lyncis is a 5th-mag. blue-white star with an 8th-mag. companion for small telescopes. In apertures of 75mm or more the brighter component is seen to have a much closer 6th-mag. companion, making 12 Lyncis a triple star.

19 Lyncis is a neat pair of 6th-mag. stars for small telescopes.

38 Lyncis is a tight pair of 4th and 6th mag. stars that provide a challenge for small telescopes because of their closeness.

41 Lyncis is to be found over the border in Ursa Major (page 222). Small telescopes show it to be an interesting triple star, consisting of components of 5th, 8th and 10th mags., arranged in a triangle.

LYRA The Lyre

A prominent constellation of the northern hemisphere of the sky, representing the harp of Orpheus; the neighbouring constellation of Cygnus is sometimes visualized as Orpheus himself.

Bright star

α (alpha) Lyrae (Vega, from the Arabic meaning stone eagle) is a brilliant blue-white star of mag. 0.0, the fifth-brightest star in the entire sky. It lies 26 l.y. away. Vega forms one corner of the Summer Triangle of three bright stars, completed by Deneb in Cygnus and Altair in Aquila.

Variable and double stars

β (beta) Lyrae is an eclipsing cream-coloured binary star that varies from mags. 3.4 to 4.3 every 12 days 22 hours. (For a comparison chart, see page 147). Small telescopes resolve β (beta) Lyrae as an attractive double star, with a blue companion of 8th mag. (In addition there are two wider 9th-mag. companions that can be seen in small telescopes.)

δ (delta) Lyrae is another double variable. Binoculars show one blue-white star, mag. 6.0, and a red giant semi-regular variable, which varies erratically between 4th and 5th mags.

continued